The Postal Confessions

UNIVERSITY
OF
MASSACHUSETTS
PRESS

Amherst

THE POSTAL CONFESSIONS

MAX GARLAND

Copyright © 1995 by
Max Garland
All rights reserved
Printed in the United States of America
LC
ISBN 0-87023-982-1
Designed by Milenda Nan Ok Lee
Set in Minion by Keystone Typesetting, Inc.
Printed and bound by Braun Brumfield, Inc.
Library of Congress Cataloging-in-Publication Data
Garland, Max, 1954–
    The postal confessions / Max Garland.
        p.   cm.
    ISBN 0-87023-982-1 (pbk. : alk. paper)
I. Title.
PS3557.A7162P67   1995   94-41649
811'.54—dc20   CIP
British Library Cataloguing in Publication data are available.

for my family

If there is a worm in the heart, & chamber it has bitten out,
I will protect that emptiness until it is large enough.
In it will be a light the color of steel
& landscape, into which the traveler might set out.

—John Anderson, "John Clare"

Acknowledgments

Poems in this collection have appeared in the following publications:

Carolina Quarterly: "Lessons from a Fifties Childhood"; "Memories of Pentecost"

Chicago Review: "For a Johnson County Snowfall"

Crazy Horse: "Dreamwork for the Elegy"

Georgia Review: "Ornament"

Gettysburg Review: "The Missiles, 1962"

Iowa Review: "Introduction to the Phenomena"; "Homage to White Bread"; "The Woman on the Road to Kamari"

Kentucky Poetry Review: "Thirst"

Louisville Review: "Baby Boom"; "Carp Remains Near Kentucky Dam"; "Strawberries"

Madison Review: "The Bombers"

Plainsong: "Apology to the Boy in the Photographs"; "Uncle"; "Reminiscence on the Nature and Cause of Flowers"; "A Brief Lecture on the Tear"; "An Oral History of the English Language"; "The Ferry from Patras"; "In the Time It Takes to Say This"; "Shoreline"

Poet and Critic: "Requiem for a Boom Town"

Poetry: "Fedoras"; "The Postal Confessions"; "Cappuccino at the Marconi Hotel in Venice"; "Revisiting the Sistine Chapel"; "Mirror"; "County Night"

Southern Poetry Review: "The Morning After"; "Outline for a Baptist History of Highway 305"

Special Report: "An Oral History of the English Language"

Zone 3: "Because You Left Me a Handful of Daffodils"; "A Barn Near the Grahamville Fork"

The author wishes to thank the National Endowment for the Arts, the Dane County Cultural Affairs Commission, and the Wisconsin Institute for Creative Writing for their support.

CONTENTS

Genealogy   1

I

Fedoras   5
An Oral History of the English Language   7
A Little Baptist Harmony, Please   8
For an Evening in Late Summer   9
A Barn near the Grahamville Fork   10
Apology to the Boy in the Photographs   12
Baby Boom   14
Homage to White Bread, Circa 1956   15
Requiem for a Boom Town   17
Sermon on the Sweet Corn   18
The Meaning of Baseball   19
The Termite Confessions   22
Uncle   24
The Postal Confessions   25
Aria for the U.S. Mail   26

II

Outline for a Baptist History of Highway 305   31
Classic Migraine on the Ferry from Ocracoke Island   32
Carp Remains near Kentucky Dam   33
Cave Country   35
Introduction to the Phenomena, Circa 1959   37
Ornament   39
The Bells   40

For an Ohio River Baptism   41
Memories of Pentecost   42
Sermon on the Heart   43
Because You Left Me a Handful of Daffodils   45
Reminiscence on the Nature and Cause of Flowers   47
Lessons from a Fifties Childhood   49
The Widow Visitations   50
County Night   52
The Missiles, 1962   54
Hydrogen   56
Initiation, 1965   57
Kegler   59

III

Self-Lecture on the 8th of September   65
The Morning After   66
The Nap Situation   67
For a Snow in Late December   68
A Little Advice for the Snow   69
A Lesson in Love   70
The Muffins   73
A Brief Lecture on the Tear   75
For a Woman in the Middle of Winter   76
For a Johnson County Snowfall   77
Mirror   79
Dressing   80
Thirst   81
Driving through Coldwater   82
In the Time It Takes to Say This   83
Strawberries   84
Dreamwork for the Elegy   87

Shoreline   88
The Ferry from Patras   89
The Woman on the Road to Kamari   90
The Bombers, A Greek Love Tale   91
Cappuccino at the Marconi Hotel in Venice   93
Revisiting the Sistine Chapel   94

The Postal Confessions

GENEALOGY

Out of the mix of mud
and the pull of the past
death is,

out of the spring rain trapped
like a damp shadow
in the clod,

*some grand*mother, father,
tattered will *arises?*

From every wet thing in the field,
every undone husk, disreputable
and sodden straw,

from all you ever lost
and never loved, until
the loss drove you down

to the place where all roots
are driven, some ghost, some grief,
slips through the gates of the alphabet—

loop and collonade, syllabics
of glottal and thrum,

until speech, or song,

until language itself seems as gilded
and superfluous

as the color of grass
the sheep graze on,
or the plow turns under,

or grows on graves
not even the rain can find.

FEDORAS

They come out of the 1940s
to be your parents. Their faces
swim and settle into clarity.
The crook of an arm. The fount
of a breast. They come from
the time before your life,
before the things that fill
your life. Before water
sprang from the faucet. Before
television loomed in the corner
and even the house cats gathered
to watch. They come from after
the war, when all the movies
were jubilant, even the sad ones
bloodless. It's as if you
were handed down to them,
as if you were a pearl
they would polish into life.
From times of great difficulty
they come, though speaking
with a deep nostalgia,
lowering the language to you
like a ladder, rung by rung.
Before *you* existed, they *are*,
which is like something
out of the Bible. Out of
their own childhoods they come
to be stricken with this,
to be stricken with time,
of which you are the immediate

symptom. Bringing their jewelry
and shaving brushes, wearing
their fedoras and hairdos,
they come to be your parents.
You have your father's eyes
someone says. But no, you
have your mother's face and eyes
is the more common opinion.
They send you wobbling out
like a top in front of them.
The wind could almost bowl
you over. You turn back
and they are dressed
like characters in a movie
or a dream. You turn back
and this is love. Your own name
sinks in and separates you.

AN ORAL HISTORY OF
THE ENGLISH LANGUAGE

Sometimes I wake up with my hillbilly voice.
I don't know why. Maybe a dream took me back.
The catalpas wilting in the heat.
The dust-devils walking the dry field.
Maybe the river was trying to shine
through the silt and accumulated years.
But when my head cleared and sleep ended,
there was only the twang of home left over,
like stubble in a milo field.

Sometimes I wake with the voice of my mother,
every syllable stretched like sorghum
or cold honey. The vowels washing over
the consonants without mercy. Every word
elongated, drenched in deliberation.
The name of my sister for instance, *Pam*,
becomes *Pay-yum*; takes two syllables,
one to release the word, the other
to call her back again.

Or sometimes I wake with my schooled tongue.
The tongue that moved away. All the *i*'s and *y*'s
precisely spoken, buttoned in their uniforms,
the cap brims set at the proper angles
of ambition. A voice clipped
and regulated, rising and falling
like the boots of a mercenary, drawn
deeper and deeper into the provinces,
hunting the stragglers of childhood down.

A LITTLE BAPTIST HARMONY, PLEASE

Here it's pronounced the same
as *hominy,* which according to the natives,
served with butter and salt, can provide a man
a hundred years of life,

if he is careful. If he is not,
it still functions as ballast
for the body. For wherever hominy
enters, it remains.

Harmony, on the other hand,
is all about leaving the body.
It takes at least two, willing
to make the trip.

For if the spirit comes down
it must be lured by music.
By separate voices wound
into a braid, then looped

into a kind of snare, which,

with eyes wide open, and for reasons
of its own, the spirit steps into,
every single time.

FOR AN EVENING
IN LATE SUMMER

My mother drawls from the porch steps.
My own name ripples and lapses

into the corn. All day near the arbor
and my tongue is the color of grapes

or the neck of a grackle. My knees
are whorled and clotted with dust.

Her voice again, loose
and drifting like a scarf.

Strange, how hunger is a weight
I wag home in my hips.

The insects grow amorous and bright.
The dark shakes off the grass and rises.

A BARN NEAR THE
GRAHAMVILLE FORK

When I was seven I'd climb into the loft,
where I could be invisible, like the Methodist
Jesus, a benign watcher of the farm.
A quarrel of crows flapped into the locusts
bordering the field. Herefords navigated
the rye. Imitating the circle of the pond,
swallows lured the insects up. While
just below, pullets scratched a living
from the hoofprints of the great sow,
twitching in her wrapper of gnats.

Then the row of empty stalls, then
the filled crib where the corn snake
grew larger by the year. A presence
we could have ended, but didn't,
and therefore twisted evil
to our advantage, I was taught.
Although I debated the point as I sat
in the loft. A fleck of hay wandered
into the sun. My dull sister, the calf,
stood in the muck near the trough.

And I wondered whose side it was right
to be on: the corn snake, coiled
into a thick rope of patience,
waiting, as still as the grain;
or the field rat I knew

would eventually scamper from his nest
of stale straw behind the rusted harrow;
the little creature whose name was filth,
but whose flaw was genuine hunger,
for which he stole the corn and died.

APOLOGY TO THE BOY
IN THE PHOTOGRAPHS

These days I don't believe in anything
that doesn't have the loss of innocence
scrawled across its forehead.

This boy, for instance, in the photographs:
black and white, curled at the edges;
posed with tricycle, with snowman,
blowing out the candles of the cake.
A boy not particularly able, as it turns out,
to find his way through the body of a man.

I don't know how to help him.
It's as if he were trapped in my ribs,
looking out, the heart tilted
like a wave above him. The mind?
All the static in the world
can't seem to form a single light.

The only way to go, it seems,
is backwards, to retrace,
which is not so much
like following a thread
as stepping into a web.

I feel for him, this boy. I just
don't know how to help him.
I don't know how to lift him

from the darkness of this body.

And even if I could save him,
even if I could lift him up,
what then? How,
and where in this world,
could I ever put him down again?

BABY BOOM

Since it was noon, Saturday, and mild,
even the town pigeons walked like taxpayers
near the market.

A Buick the size of a barge unmoored
itself from the curb in front of the jeweler's:
nine miles to the gallon, and still
there was too much future to use.

The sun grazed the chrome of the parked cars
from the top of its arc over town, thinning
the shadow of the floodwall, spelling
abundance across the windows of the bank;

while at Kresge's lipstick counter
the high school girls were busy
ignoring the farm boys loitering
near the fountain, though every mouth
they tried said *marry me.*

HOMAGE TO WHITE BREAD, CIRCA 1956

It was called *Bunny Bread* in Kentucky;
from the cellophane, a cartoon rabbit
aimed a smile at my sister and me.

This was before the cult of the body,
before whole wheat, before fiber.
This was bread as white
as the bedsheets tugging at the line,
as white as the soul ascending;

as insubstantial as the fields
passing across the windows of cars,
yet bread reattaining, in the throat,
the consistency of wet dough;

which we loved, my sister and I,
a rare agreement, in fact,
as we clawed through the rivalries,
children of such bread.

This was the bread of television,
of styrofoam, of prayer
refined to the point of memory,
such as, "Give us this day
our daily . . ."

White bread, snowfall, fleece;

this was bread to soften the blow
when the time to remember came.
Bread of persuasion. Bread like a filter
through which only the innocents pass,
bread of the hand that writes it so.

REQUIEM FOR A BOOM TOWN

It was Sunday, 1957, and the parking lot
of the Episcopal Church
was the best time a tail-fin ever had.

The sunlight fractured itself, car after car,
each one sleeker than the one before;
cars the size of small living rooms,
each one more radiant;

as if the families merely waited
in the church, killing time,
while the real worship
was parked in the lot,

was the sun on the grillwork, or shapely
along the fenders,

or in the names of the animals
emblazoned above the trunk latches.

The real worship was in the sound
of the car door closing, heavy
as a vault, the settling in,
and that moment of silence
just before he turned her over,

and felt himself, the wife, the son,
the daughter, lifted in the glittering wave
of all a man could ever want.

SERMON ON THE SWEET CORN

Sweet because it's a sugar built of days,
spring rain, a parched leaf,
and a windfall of pollen. *Sweet*

because it's difficult to gather; the leaves
are a gauntlet to walk in late summer.
And difficult to eat, on the cob,

requiring a lack of pretense, an abandonment
of manners, a partial ignorance,
a fundamental hunger. *Sweet*

because of the money, and the memory
of want: the watery soups of childhood,
the dust bowl at the end of the drought.

Or *sweet* as a term of endearment,
as in *sweetheart* or *sweet Jesus,*
which may also refer to taste, of course:

the physical sensation of a lover,
or a Jesus, like honey on the tongue;
a single drop, a simple pleasure,

that nevertheless continues
in the world like corn,
and out of the world like joy.

THE MEANING OF BASEBALL

We sit on the bench like shy freight,
like timid whippersnappers. One by one
are called forward, our names barked
into the air. We swing

before the ball even leaves the coach's hand,
swing when it's halfway home, swing
as it rolls past the catcher,
crawls to a stop like a bug in the dust.

We try techniques of our own invention,
throwing the bat *at* the ball,
the bat spinning like a fan blade,
the poor man, someone's father,
flattened on the mound.

Sometimes it's ourselves we hit
as the bat comes awkwardly around,
our faces winding into tiny knots
of unfallen tears. Occasionally,

eventually, there is the wooden sound
of impact, like an accident.
The ball dribbles forth, or even flies.

And the feeling is exactly
what we feel years later
the first time the heart misfires,
sputters a few beats, then rights
itself. In other words,

the empty space inside the body.

Summer moves along. Some of us outshine
the others, the wheat separated
rather bluntly from the chaff.
Grounders thump against our chests,

fly balls descend upon us
like strangers we've been warned against.
We've been in school enough to know
the rising moon above the field

is a ball, the earth is a ball,
the seasons themselves, a kind of ball.

One night, standing under the lights,
we suddenly know exactly what will happen.
For no reason on earth, lean left,
take three quick steps and begin to run
as if from something faceless in a dream.

Someone yells *back,* someone *stop.*
The voices register, but fail to matter
(wheat from the chaff) for we have discovered
the tiny scale of destiny. The ball is a smudge,

a shadow, something floating under the eyelids.
We are heading for a place the night
itself has decided. Our legs pump,
a hand shoots out, the ball hangs

in the thinnest part of the webbing.
Roberto, someone screams from the stands,
meaning *Clemente,* the greatest
and strangest player of our day.

Later, much older, we'll spend hours
on bleachers, reading papers,
in front of televisions, not knowing
we are looking for this moment,

which for reasons of physics alone,
can never return. Though it will occur to us
at times—opening an envelope, lifting a couch,
or just before the anesthetic takes hold,

that there is a net below our lives,
that we can know what will happen,
the way a circle is foretold
by the first few degrees of an arc,
that knowledge can break our fall.

Though it may not be true, of course,
it *is* the meaning of baseball,
as taught to us as children,

as we open our envelope, as we lift
our couch, as we lie on our gurney
counting backwards from ten.

THE TERMITE CONFESSIONS

It wasn't the worst job I'd had, wasn't
sweeping parking lots, or sponging toilets,
wasn't digging graves in packed clay.
But it was crawling in the dark
beneath houses, through generations
of cobwebs, cast-off snake skins,
brick shards, with my flashlight
and termite hammer, tapping for rot,
for the crumble of wood that meant
they were there, legions of them—
insatiable nymphs, blind white workers;
while above me the house sagged,
the duct-work flexed, the worried owner
scraped a kitchen chair across linoleum
as I inched my way along, belly-up
in the realm of the tiny beasts
tunneling themselves into the galleries
of the floorboards, mining the wood
for cellulose, sucking it out like honey
until even the oak grew papery,
dry as puffball,

and eventually drew the house down,
though it could take a century or two.
Time is on the side of appetite,
I found myself deciding; and maybe
it was the damp, the must, the mold,
the torn scarves of spiderwebs I wore,
but I felt in strange cahoots,
noticed a pull as I crawled

under the nail heads and grouted pipes.
Sometimes even switched off the light
and just lay beneath a riddled beam
and felt myself crossing over,
the way secret agents must feel
in the arms of their informants,
or even the best executioners
eventually come to feel—that shift
in perspective, allegiance,
as if some small dark love
were gnawing its way inside,
and the last thing I wanted
was light.

UNCLE
—for Sam Bowling

You knew better than this. You could have become
the strange but lovable uncle who never married,
never puzzled a wife with children, puzzled themselves,
unguided by the wobbly light of the word, *Father.*

Now your son sleepwalks the mild adventure
you've given him. Your daughter follows your voice,
the safe reach into sleep. Your wife leans toward
the timely skeleton she knows you see
at the heart of things. So many ways to inhabit
your mistakes. Sometimes it hardly matters
that you live the wrong life. But there you are,

who should be buying souvenirs
for nieces and nephews, those strange
complicated toys that wind up weathered
in driveways and backyards, but rise again
in the grown memory. Small clues
down the back way to childhood.

This should be happening now:
you standing at your brother's door
saying goodbye, with your suitcase
of clean clothes and intricately folded maps,
making promises his children have learned
you will keep. People mention loneliness.
They wonder if you miss their lives.
Then you hold your brother,
then you kiss his wife.

THE POSTAL CONFESSIONS

The sorting machine whirs like the blades of a fan.
You could fall asleep if it weren't for the money,
if it weren't for the fact that the work
is already much deeper than sleep,
and what could you fall into lower than life
you never intended, yet inhabit
like the rumble in the conveyor's constant moan.
The strange thing is, hardly anyone writes anymore,
yet the tonnage builds and builds. Hardly anyone
spills even a grain of his life in a letter,
yet the machines whir and jam, the bundles
threaten to topple, the mail cases bulge
with billing and the inky brightness of sales pitch.
You could fall asleep if it weren't for the third cup
of vending machine coffee, which resembles in color,
texture, and taste, the silted waters of the Ohio in spring,
which is why they built the town in the first place,
to drink the waters of the river, to burden
the long twisted back of the river with barges
and bridges, to sit in the slump of afternoon
watching the sun float down from white to yellow
to red to maroon, the last few gulls raking the far
shore, as if even the shadows were richer there.

ARIA FOR THE U.S. MAIL

Some days it's all the hope you get,
this postal froth and cataract, letters
spilling and tumbling down the conveyor,
tern white, thin as flounder.
Above the flutter of typography
and penmanship, the bright stamp
depicting a wild bird, a suffragette,
the inventor of the threshing machine;
the stamp like a tiny sail, blown jagged
by the bleak winds of cancellation.
Some days as you stand at the sorter—
your pale blue shirt, knee-high socks,
the fact that any word reaches anyone
seems miracle enough, that memory
has a slim, but measurable weight,
that thought flies above you
in the night, over the sooted rooftops,
bales and bundles of it, higher
than breath or weather.
That a letter ever lands on earth
seems enough, that you can
hold it, sniff it, steam it open,
even clutch it to your breast
in some private operatic gesture.
And we're not talking the love letters
of Keats here, or the fifteenth epistle
of Paul. It may be no more, in fact,
than a dashed-off note, a utility bill,
an invitation to a wedding
between two people everyone knows

should never have met. But still,
who's to say? What with the ground
not so solid under you, and the world
on its flight through practically nothing,
there is this tiny message
from beyond yourself, for better
or worse, in its own shy way,
demanding an answer.

PART
TWO

PART
TWO

PART
TWO

OUTLINE FOR A BAPTIST HISTORY
OF HIGHWAY 305

The meadowlark nesting
between the tines of the cultivator,

or the black snake I diced into eternity
with a long-handled hoe in 1957,

are the choices this same field
flashes back for me, thirty years later:

one of compassion, we left the birds alive;
and one of biblical wrath,

swinging again and again
from the safe end of an arc of justice.

Seven years old. The black snake in pieces.
My first real taste of smiting.

The meadowlark safe in the field.

CLASSIC MIGRAINE ON THE
FERRY FROM OCRACOKE ISLAND

It's too far from home to be without a head
or I'd throw half into the water
and half to the streamer of laughing-gulls
flapping backward from the boat.
But now the half I'd toss to the gulls
is reminding the half I'd give to the water
how it's my own fault, this pain;
how the doctor clearly told me
to avoid chocolate, red wine, pelicans,
and ferries between small southern islands,
especially during azalea time.

God, it's such a bright, warped filter
the gulls descend. If I weren't
so sick I'd promise to be happy;
the sunlight scorched into the tail-feathers
and the borders of the wings.
They could be angels up there,
if it weren't for the constant hunger;
and even then they could be angels
if they had better manners;
and maybe even then, a few of them
could be angels, if it weren't
for the little black executioner's hoods
they wear, the hysterical laughing and crying,
the waves pulling the islands apart.

CARP REMAINS
NEAR KENTUCKY DAM

When the tail-fin lost its will
he swam an afternoon of circles,
a lake as small as his strength,
until the waves broke into gravel
here at Hillman Ferry.

Not a real ferry anymore, just
a shadow crossing the thread of river
hidden in the lake.

Not even a real lake, just
a broad stain of sky and water
swept over the marginal farms,
even swallowing a town or two,
everyone paid off years ago
in brick houses with carports.

He might have been a week's work
for the fish-crows and flies;
all but the barest architecture
scooped away; a few tough shingles
on a web of filament and bone,
a faint holdout of aroma.

I once swam over a town here, though

I couldn't tell you much about it,
just an aisle of green water,
a glazed look about the waves.

Much like the look he must have had
near the end, when he had a look.
What else is left to say?

Maybe I should mention the little
empty socket that held the world.
Maybe I should wonder where it went.
Maybe it takes a deeper kind of witness
than I'm ready to be

to remember the carp in a way
that means it didn't happen;
or if it did, doesn't matter;
or if it does, is for the best.
Maybe that would be a fish
the world he lost could feed on.

CAVE COUNTRY

Under the farms were the rivers
where the worn-out snow lived,
the shy rain, the pale
eyeless cave fish.

Under the plow
turning up the furrows,
under the early blades of corn,
whole nations of bats hung
like charred and wilted leaves.

Under the gravestones
memory grew less particular;
every year it was harder
to say whose life was whose,
whose ancestor, whose enemy.
Between mowings the honey-
suckle grew fearless, creeping
over the Christian names.

Under nightfall, under the covers,
under a boy's flickering eyelids
was a kind of cave
where nothing could be depended upon
to remain itself, where even fear
seemed fluid, if not downright
delicious.

Under the threat of daylight

the bats streamed home
to the mouth of the hill.

The mother stirred the house alive.
Under the sound of his own name,
the boy took up his only body.
Under the morning, the river ran.
Under the waking, the blind fish swam.

INTRODUCTION TO THE PHENOMENA, CIRCA 1959

It was all those weather predictions
and local politics; who made money,
whose wife left with whom,

combined with the opened bottles
of tonic and dye, that eventually
stained the windows of the barbershop
green—

a light cast outward
over the sidewalk and street;
an eerie shade, like stumbling
into someone else's dream.

It was simple human loneliness
that swept the same piece of paper
down Broadway every evening;
stopping to press the curb, here;
wrapping around a meter, there.

It was the will of God the pigeons
didn't fall from the ledges
above the Columbia Theater.
They looked as heavy as mallards
up there, such waddlers
and constant complainers.
In other words, made for love.

Such lovers, in fact, sometimes

we had to shoot them down.

A few hours after the roosting
an assortment of dry goods men,
grocers, and sheriff's deputies
loaded their son's pellet rifles

and before morning the dead
would be gathered.

And before a year had passed
the pigeons were back,
neither fewer, nor wiser;
maybe even the same pigeons.

And everything below
began to acquire the same patina,
the same splatterings and leavings of love,
spilling over the cornices
and acanthus leaves, the awnings
and facades; the same pigeons,
the same grey-white frosting
we killed them the first time for.

ORNAMENT

Somewhere between the end of the river
and the discovery of television
rust froze the weather vane
into a permanent southwest wind,
the lane of the summer storms.

Almost every day another thing we trusted
began to ornament our lives:
the smell of kerosene, the well-rope,
clatter of the milk jar, riffle of the hymnal.

When the cattle market dove, the pond
lay in the field like a bright stone
dropped from a ring.

The hens became frivolous
and changed into white camellias
strutting the wind along the fencerow

about the time we discovered
we were paying the hired man, Tom,
for work we could have done ourselves;

and though he was poor as ever,
it was only out of kindness
he took our money at all.

THE BELLS

The bells flush the pigeons from the shoulders
of Saint Francis, from the ledges, sills
and false balustrades of the only Catholic
church in town. As far as they're concerned,
the pigeons, that is, rock is rock. Whether
mortared or carved or slowly accreted from
the tiny fluttering bodies of the Paleozoic.
Cliff, quarry, or small town cathedral,
it's all the same steep outlook, the same
convoluted and chiseled perch from which
to launch one's own rescue, which is what
the pigeons do as the bells call Mass.
They simply shuffle for a beat on their
embarrassingly thin age-of-the-reptile legs,
then lean and fall into the warm air reflected
upward from the hollows of the street,
which carries them in a great flapping wheel,
then a tightening arc, then a slow glide back
through the wilted thunder of the bells
to the rock that was always home.

FOR AN OHIO RIVER BAPTISM

It was late summer, so the children
were marrying each other again;
the girls just old enough
to make their own dresses
carried the babies
of the boys with cars.

Because the afternoon was ending,
there was a spill of copper on the waves,
and if you glanced quickly enough
from the river, the town windows swung
like keys on a chain. Because

it was 1927, the iceman
was worried, and the horse
that knew the milk route by heart
was still a conspicuous absence.

Since it was Sunday, when
the wind died, the men
pulled out their handkerchiefs,
the women used their hats as fans,
the Christians stood hip-deep
in the water. A coal barge
dwindled. The river birds
swayed in the honey.

MEMORIES OF PENTECOST

I had an uncle who healed by faith
and drove a Lincoln. Smack in the middle
of the forehead with the palm of his hand
and the eyes wobbled in their sockets,
sound like a ribbon unfurled from the tongue.
It might have been Hebrew.
It might have been Chickasaw.
It may have had something to do
with marrying cousins. Who's to say
it wasn't the blow of grace itself?

The organist beating the hymn
like a bad child. The ceiling fan
spinning as if the roof might fly away.

And even if the spirit missed me
by an eyelash, a whisker, a country mile,
even if Sunday after Sunday I dodged
the white arrow that pierced the true apostles,
it was enough to know it was somewhere
in the family, somewhere in my uncle,
flapping like a wild bird in his chest
as he touched them, as he let them go,
the organ swooping down like a train at a crossing
as he danced his little dance—one step,
then a wiggle, *Sweet Jesus,* sweet jangle,
the keys to the Lincoln alive in his pocket.

SERMON ON THE HEART

If death is incorporated, curled
like an embryo in the living heart,
sleeping, though not that soundly;
in fact, unfurling slightly
as he sleeps, like the building
of a yawn;

if my heart is a house death outgrows
a chamber at a time,
passing through the stages
toward the personal, from *death*
to *my death*,

from abstract darkness
to the pale hope of syringes,
and the lampshade tilted away
because there's only so much
even those who loved me
would really want to see;

if that's what death is,
a living thing
that can't help itself,
that can't help but grow
out to the end of my body:
this hand, the tips
of these two fingers;

then death is doomed

unless some crumb remains,
some morsel bearing my name,
a touchstone, or memory,
for the time when death
has wandered enough,
or stumbled onto loneliness,
or the hunger and thirst
begin to build again,
and there's nothing left for death
but to look for me, to find me,
to raise me up, unless
there is no death,
and make me live again.

BECAUSE YOU LEFT ME A
HANDFUL OF DAFFODILS

I suddenly thought of Brenda Hatfield, queen
of the 5th grade, Concord Elementary.
A very thin, shy girl, almost
as tall as Audrey Hepburn,
but blond.

She wore a dress based upon the principle
of the daffodil: puffed sleeves,
inflated bodice, profusion
of frills along the shoulder blades
and hemline.

A dress based upon the principle of girl
as flower; everything unfolding, spilling
outward and downward: ribbon, stole,
corsage, sash.

It was the only thing I was ever
elected. A very short king.
I wore a bow tie, and felt
like a third-grader.

Even the scent of the daffodils you left
reminds me. It was a spring night.
And escorting her down the runway
was a losing battle, trying to march
down among the full, thick folds
of crinoline, into the barrage of her

father's flashbulbs, wading
the backwash of her mother's
perfume: scared, smiling,
tiny, down at the end
of that long, thin, Audrey Hepburn arm,
where I was king.

REMINISCENCE ON THE NATURE
AND CAUSE OF FLOWERS

Flowers followed women
through all I remember of childhood.

From the border of petunias and marigolds
around the porch, to the print dress

my grandmother wore. From the scent
of my least favorite aunt, to the blush

of my mother's cheek. Jonquils
on the table, African violets on the sill.

Even the paper gardenias in my sister's crown,
queen of the second grade.

A man might own the farm.
A man might possess

the entire kingdom of vegetables.
My grandfather did. Might condescend

to till the roses. Might even carefully mow
around the young tulips and irises.

But it would only be a spell left over
from sleeping with a woman. No man:

father, grandfather, man-in-the-moon,

could be the cause of flowers;

not a single snowball, lilac, crepe
myrtle, mimosa; and never,

never the japonica.

LESSONS FROM A
FIFTIES CHILDHOOD

A woman grows plush as a pillow.
A man gets lean, like jerky,
as if smoked by his own tobacco.

A cigarette passes for language—
crack of flame cupped in the hand,
slow draw of thought, flick, waft,

the little red bead by which time
burns down, but never quite to the tongue.
Nothing gets quite to the tongue.

A woman is washing and drying a dish,
a long calendar of dishes, drying
all the way down to the squeak

where her own face begins to appear,
vague, opalescent,
in a rim of painted flowers.

THE WIDOW VISITATIONS

Her chihuahua had a single tooth
with which to count the hours
until Sunday,

the saucers of boiled chicken
appearing like sunrise
or moonrise.

Did his small business
on the spread pages
of the local daily, loosed

his three gull-like cries
at the gravel
stirring in the drive,

wound like a water bug
around the dumpling
ankles of the lady visitors

who built of the afternoon
a temple of complaints,
composed a litany

of stiffenings
and downright seizures,
spells and insomnias

until even the furniture

began to tick off time,
the first jolts of the cicadas

sifted in through the screen
and goodbye and God-bless-you
at the kitchen door

to the tune of tiny claws
tapping across linoleum,
the poor thing

dancing as best he could.

COUNTY NIGHT

My aunt is knitting a doily, or is it
a wafer, or is it a snowflake
that will never melt?

Or is it the flitting of winter light
itself she has snared, and entangles?
Or maybe the riddled white wing

of a moth? According to *King James,*
cooling like a black loaf on the lampstand,
it's 6,000 years since the birth of light,

though it seems that long since morning.
There is no television this far out.
There is no uncle, the uncles

all swept from their fifties
by the postwar epidemic of worry.
There is something slightly reptilian

in the African violet on the sill.
Even a sleepy child could see
the tail-flick shadow,

the belly-softness of the leaf.
A clock ticks like a hanging man,
like bootheels scraping the barn-

loft, as I lay me down

beneath afghan and comforter.
And as I sleep, or if I wake,

the doily unfurls from the lap
of my aunt, or is it some papery
funeral flower? Or is it

some strange new flag, in the blown
and rippled moment of dream,
I can almost count the stars on?

THE MISSILES, 1962

It was the heyday of the platter, the disc,
the grooves cut deep and mysteriously benign,
so that if you danced with a boy,
the dance spun like the record itself
or the world spinning both of you.
And whatever they put in the perfume
infiltrated the shyness, so that his heart,
such as it was, fresh from boyland,
clean as a stone, was soon scratched tighter
than the platter, so maybe not so benign.
For not only was the song etched in,
but the brush of thighs, the damp
hand in hand, the whole swept
and cantilevered industry of your hair
from which wafted a bright chemical
and yet vaguely lunar aroma;
the moment pressed into keeping,
notched into a pattern that eventually,
a week, a month, matured into the will
to live for each other, or even die.
For wouldn't he gamble a life for you?
And didn't the record turn relentlessly
in love? nailing the beat to the palms
of your hands, thumping like a fist
at the breastbone; helpless love,
hopeless love, storm of love, sea
of love. And wasn't he the one
you imagined when they tested the sirens
for the bomb drills? the roar sweeping

in a widening circle over the school,
the screech lapsing and returning as you
crouched in the cafeteria. And wasn't
he the reason you covered your face
to save it from the imploding glass?
but at the same time not taking it
all that seriously, but at the same time
if only an island were left alive,
wouldn't he be the one you'd want there?
the two of you, the world of you;
nothing but the lapping of waves
stretched around and around you.
Sad, of course; tragic, of course.
But wouldn't it seem somewhat
familiar? And wouldn't it be
almost enough? the milky reaches
of haze, the stippled horizon;
the two of you, the world of you.

HYDROGEN

A balloon, a bomb, a drop of water.
The skin around the sun burning outward.
You are truly next to nothing,
and yet everywhere. So neighborly,
so eager to combine:
when oxygen decided to swim,
you only asked *how far;*
when tears needed a catalyst,
you solemnly stepped forth.
In every cell, plant or animal,
it's just not the same without you.
It's not the same ocean or body;
it's not the rain or snow. And still,
such a vulnerable element:
just a proton huddled
under the wavering attentions
of a lone electron. A body com-
posed mainly of the distance
between you. A fragile marriage
which, if it ends, may end badly,
and your loss breed a loneliness so deep,
as tiny as you are, the whole world
withdraws in consolation.

INITIATION, 1965

Because a boy must murder something,
because a boy must be implicated,
we were shooting the doves
with a pattern of shot as wide
and heartless as the hand of God,
because one of us would be sent to war
in a country he couldn't find on the map,
because one of us would stay alive
by a series of academic maneuvers,
because one of us would remember
how the wind flapped through the blades
of milo, how we baited the field,
crouched in the dirt of the roadside.

You have to lead a dove, you have
to aim for the next move he makes,
which is a move into nothing,
which is a shattering of iridescent
feathers, a limp body
none of us was hungry for.

Because a little blood on the hands
is good for a boy, a little extra
meanness might save his life,
we were shooting the doves.
The hitch in their flight,
the unpredictable swerving
made it almost seem fair
because we were terrified
of the recoil, and the bruises

kept deepening in the hollows
of our right shoulders
as we shot the doves,
because we drove our father's cars,
because we were our father's sons.
The river was slate-grey, murmured
and lapped into the willows
that marked the state-line
that bordered the field
where we were shooting the doves
because a boy must murder something,
because a boy must be implicated.

KEGLER

Even before the middle ages
the monks knew bowling was holy.

Being monks, they rolled a stone
toward a single club; a *kegel,*
it was called.

Seven thousand years ago, a boy
was entombed near Memphis, his
bowling gear sealed with him.

Speaking of faith, my father,
with a three-quarter backswing
and the spin of a perfect wrist.
would fling the ball two thin boards
from the gutter,

the *Ebonite* hooking as it flew,
trailing away and yet leaning
inward, with only the slightest
rumble of complaint.

It was soon after the war.
No one was killing anyone.
A thin smoke rose from the filter-
tips. Emblazoned across the shirts

were the names of local repair shops
for newly imagined appliances.

I could barely lift the ball.
Sixteen pounds. Like something
from the Shiloh battlefield
we visited one spring.

The lacquered pins, like plenty,
clattered around us.

In the third century, being monks,
they would prop the huge club
in a corner of the monastery.
If a peasant rolled his stone
and felled it, all was fine.
If the worshiper missed, the fault
was sin, and he was advised
to lead a better life.

When it happens right, you know it
the instant the ball is released,
the body posed like an ornament
on the hood of an old Mercury.
Not a single pin falls alone.
It's as if the strike occurred
from the inside of the cluster,
as if the ball were a coincidence,
a mere reminder for the pins
to fall and be swept

into that brief, clean horizon

from which my father would stride,
fist clenched in triumph, blue cords
straining in the wrist and forearm,

like the veins in my own wrist
as I write this to remember,
twisting it slightly, admittedly,
for love,

the way the ball itself hurried
and twisted, heavy and black
as the holes
they had not yet discovered
in space,

black as the brand new moon,
not a living soul had touched.

PART THREE

SELF-LECTURE ON THE
8TH OF SEPTEMBER

Beauty has broken into the watchworks,
the four-o'clocks bloom at sunrise,

staying open all morning. Five petals
part for the hummingbird, six tongues

of pollen rise. I know it's not much.
I know it's still possible to be unhappy,

or broken, or locked in a darkness
no flower can solve, no word can.

But it doesn't seem possible now
to ignore the scent of them, the stray

whiff of all those fragile bodies
giving themselves to the hour,

the wrong hour, the first hour
that will have them, the first

dutiful bee, the first cold
touch of the wasp.

THE MORNING AFTER

The morning after the first clean wind of fall,
we wake in a tangle of sheets. The morning
swings from the blood, tightens in the breath.
Our sleep is still loose upon our bodies.

Almost overnight, the catalpa leaves
have turned their attention to falling.
Grounded in the first wash of arctic air,
they prepare to crack like campfires
around our feet.

We find ourselves moving in the light
of new instructions, breathing deeper,
walking faster. We sense an edge,
and a thought lacing the shadow
of that edge, a thought we recognize,
have held many times before—

if this was the year for our lives to occur,
the wind pulls grey into the hedge,
they should be occurring, even now.

THE NAP SITUATION

I wake up with the intelligence of moss,
and not the brightest of mosses at that.
I study the stitching of the bedsheets
with a drowsy version of awe. I notice
the shifting patterns of lint held
in the sunlight. Only minutes away
from the seamlessness of sleep
and already there's an autumn chill,
a tangle of shadows, a passel of dying
leaves at the windowpane. I'm un-
prepared for the profusion of things,
each with its own little spirit, its own
little spiel. The boundary between sloth
and pointless attention to detail
grows murky. A pencil rests uneasily
on a sill. A book stifles a cough.
A geranium pauses for emphasis.
The longer I'm awake, the more
they arrive, the separate things,
the particulars, with their hats
in their hands like mendicants,
like babies on the doorstep,
like penniless relatives
with stories so farflung and desolate
I'd need a heart of stone
not to listen.

FOR A SNOW IN
LATE DECEMBER

This is the snow that turned
like a key in the night, that twisted
in the hollow of the cloud,

cold and blind. This is the air

that set foot in the void,
and nevertheless came back, winter
woven like a coat around it.

These are the ashes of which
our footprints are made, and the wind
that gave way to the glare.

This is the snow that tried to memorize
the spring rain, much too late,
and lost heart, and began to lie,

or at least elaborate. This is the white
the rain would have wanted, argues the snow
over Davenport Street, shaping itself

into petals, into lace, into the windows
of tiny cathedrals, falling slowly
through the net of the streetlamp.

A LITTLE ADVICE
FOR THE SNOW

I think the snow needs a little rest now.
I think the snow is tired
of skating the borders of water.
I think the snow has heard
just about all he needs to hear
of the arguments of wind and ice.

A little rest. A good night's sleep.
A patch of lawn. A few cedars.
Maybe the slope of a porch roof
Maybe even a beholder, someone
to notice those first, few,
tentative flakes.

I think the snow needs a little less strength,
a degree or two. I think the snow
needs faith enough to fall
into nobody's arms tonight. I think
the snow should close his eyes now,
and let whatever he sees there
begin to happen.

A LESSON IN LOVE

By February I find myself
speaking to common house plants.
It's that deep into the winter.
Tell me, fern. Yes, Brother geranium?
Though it's not exactly a brother,
the geranium; both sexes rise
in the same blood red flower.

It was the almost elderly Colette
who wrote about finally
escaping from being a woman.
Could I say the same about
being a man? And what
is the thing that escapes?
The blossom beyond gender?

The snow reflects the sunlight upward,
an extra dosage for the ficus
and schefflera. How close to love
is ordinary sunlight?

And if you had to choose between them?
I wonder, unfortunately aloud,

what it's like for the plants

when the nitrogen kicks in.
Is *giddiness* the right word?

And those trace elements in the loam,
do they drift up like daydreams,
or brief inexplicable ambitions.

Colette would have been able to describe
the blue of the sky today—
not as deep as cobalt, or indigo,
nor as slippery as turquoise;
neither the blue of eggshell
nor flame.

The best I can say is
it's a sky that seems more available
than it is, a beauty you imagine,
wrongly, you could gather in your arms.

I like to think this is not quite
craziness, merely February.
I like to think there's some
internal equinox

when the mind grows most brittle,
its chances of breaking, or healing,
exactly the same.

From this point, desire

advances a little each day,
though by such tiny increments,
with such botanical slowness,

you'd have to be a leaf to notice,
a root, a stem, some late
winter blossom, neither
man nor woman.

THE MUFFINS

I take them as a sign of hope,
in spite of the leftover rain
in the redbuds,

in spite of the lurk of clouds
and the sad, milky repetitions
of the city fountain.

They remind me of schoolchildren
lined up under the slanted glass,
or homely beauty contestants

sugar-glazed, inflated
beyond reason, fatally smitten
by their own dreamy contours;

the youngest, still warm
from the oven; the elderly,
darkly stoic, stiffened with patience,

the shape of the muffin tin
haunting them
like a dominant gene.

I take it as a sign of hope
that, unburdened by protein
or conscience,

innocent of nutrient

or memory, the muffins
have concocted a life for themselves;

surviving, like mushrooms,
by mistaking themselves
for flowers.

I find myself strangely moved
and lifted
by such errors:

the aroma of muffins,
their unlikely blossoms,
their brief and airy sweetness.

A BRIEF LECTURE ON THE TEAR

Here's where the young sea practices
its way around the world. Here
in the continual film over the eye.

Which reminds me how few tears
ever really fall, one in millions.
The rest retreat like tiny waves

or simply wash back and forth
in the tide across the cornea,
having nothing to do with sadness.

So the world is seen through
the thinnest of oceans, a petal
of oil and seawater on every eye.

And whatever face or flower
we turn to, is anchored
in that distortion

between the slim grace of salt
and the blink of the eye
that washes it away.

FOR A WOMAN IN THE
MIDDLE OF WINTER

A long time I lived there,
in the town of the way your hair
fell. A long time

I lay like a novice
under my own heartbeat,
practicing. Since it was winter,

the snow was spilling at the window's feet.
A long time I tried not to think;
maybe never to think. Strange,

how an instant will round itself
into a kind of toy, a glass globe
in the cup of your hand,

and when you shake it, the snow rises,
twists, and falls. Strange,

how the slope of your shoulders
and back, was the very shape
taken by the snow,

and the more of it that fell,
the more human it became,
the more it drifted and burned,
and the more I loved you.

FOR A JOHNSON COUNTY SNOWFALL

I'd settle for a paradise like this,
that kept falling apart
and regathering, that slowed
time, faltered
and hung like the weight of grace
on the houses.

I'd settle for a paradise
that folded like a white book
over the scrawl of underbrush
and twigs, that simplified
the landscape, absolving
the roads of destination.

A few birds tag along
in a rich, grey wind.
The trees are pared
to a minimal faith.

Isn't there already a place
where *blessing* and *snow*
are the same word?

I'd settle for such a paradise,
that you could gather by the handful,
though it might soon begin to burn
with the same cold knack
the winter stars have.

I'd settle for a paradise

that could be fashioned into a man,
however temporary, or comical:
a cocked hat, a pair
of ordinary stones for his eyes;
a paradise that nevertheless
could spread its spindly arms
as wide as the night was bitter,
as the wind was ice, and whirled,
and swept, and sang like a blade.

MIRROR

Every morning you search this face
as if sleep were an act of contrition,
from *conterere*—to bruise, to grind,
to rub away; as if sleep worked
the way weather works on stone
to give it the shape of time.

You search this face
to see if doubt has been dislodged
from the notorious eyebrows,
those condescenders, those qualifiers;
to see if irony has been banished
from the lay of the lips.

You study this every morning.
Touch this face with your hands
to feel the bones, the honest bones—
the seam of the mandible,
the orbits of the eyes.

You rub the eyes, little lamps.
Wish deep into the blackest part
for daylight to arrive.

DRESSING

You have to dress this body now,
which in the scale of things is not so grand;
neither as curvaceous or swift as a planet,
nor as staunch as a tree at the window.

In your considered opinion, the green
would be nice, to offset the worry,
maybe whip up the want.

There is a certain tactic in the matter of buttons,
how many to leave undone. The one? The two?
How much of the throat do you bare today?
All the way down to the breastbone?

You pull them on, cottons and blends,
fibers invented by better students than you,
spun in vats, in vials.

The body is a temple, someone
read to you as a child,
but you know the body is a child,
always, even aging.

You have to wrap him up, swaddle,
tuck, zip him in.
The memory of believing otherwise,
the only temple now.

THIRST

It's a small, physical prayer for water
in the form of a crumbling leaf
where the tongue was,

or the throat spun of chalk and a dry weed,
or the breath ground to powder.

Or a synonym for desire in general:
to crave, need, rather badly want.

Or the source of certain dreams,
as well as the reason for waking,
groping the dark hallway to the faucet
as if to fill what sleep deserted.

Or, according to death-bed witnesses,
often among the last words spoken,
a form of it, at least, triggered
by dehydration. For example,

in the case of Jesus, quoted late
in the book of John, far beyond
the help of actual water, pulling
the reader forward like rain.

DRIVING THROUGH COLDWATER

It comes and it comes back:
the fescue climbing the hill
as carefully as the light;
the inevitable Holsteins tethered
to the gift of hunger, drifting slightly,
as if they had been placed there,
models of gravity.
We pass through Viola
to Coldwater to Stella; the sun
hunts the southwest horizon.
The land doesn't mean a thing,
but lends itself to the wave
of houses along the road.
An old man nods from a porch
and we enter the local wisdom,
and the forgetting, and the losing
of powers.

IN THE TIME IT TAKES TO SAY THIS

You lift the hat, set the brim, descend
the three steps, feel the left knee
fade, then hold. Turning to the hayfield,
flattened here and there by the wind,
you think of vague, enormous animals
quietly walking that field all night,
your protectors. You're that old.
Old as the post-oak, blocking dawn.
In both of you, the grain deepens;
the strength at the core uses itself
in gusts. Now you remember night's leaves
tapping around the house; now the shadow
circles under the brim, the halo's brother,
moving as you move.

STRAWBERRIES
—for Rayford Simmons

Whatever is truly delicious
cripples,

according to a local Baptist proverb.
Whatever bides its life

under the leaves, patiently
undoing the bitter

green knot of itself, swelling outward,
deepening, reddening. Whatever ripens

in the sun, shaping itself
into a tiny version of the heart,

the sweetness at the berry's core
leaking slowly through the flesh.

We had nearly a half-acre to pick,
my grandfather and I, crawling

or stooping through the long rows.
Not much passing between us—

the faint snapping of the fruit
from the stem, the occasional

judgment of cigar smoke

trailing back to where I lagged,

knees stained almost to blossoms; the low vines

teaching the body to bend. The arc
of my grandfather's back, for example,

repeated the story of strawberry gathering,
spring after spring. Whatever is delicious

draws the man from the body, is the proverb,
coaxing the long, elderly nerve

through all the meandering hoops
of the spine. Until

after a while, my grandfather
thought it would be a good idea

to rest there. He thought
it would be a good idea to lie down

among the berries. According
to the Baptists, whatever it is

invites us, can almost taste us

near the end. He thought

it would be a good idea to sleep
down in the cool shadows

of the berry vines. Just for a while,
my grandfather thought. Just until

his mind was sweetness.
Just until his body was straw.

DREAMWORK FOR THE ELEGY

Sometimes you just go
down into a valley,
and there are white horses,
you can see them
through the mist.
And there are pine trees,
two rows, someone
planted them and died.
Good. You take another step.

There is always a hawk,
object of envy,
moving without moving;
and a river, and the dark
and the light changing lanes
over the river.

You begin to feel at home.
The longer the shadows
the more you recognize,
until you can recite
the next step blind,
until the instant
simplifies itself;
the mist clears,
the white horses are kind.
You knew they would be.

SHORELINE

Here is a rock shaped
like a corrupted bowling trophy.
And here is one clenched in a root.
And here is a boulder, his offspring
around him, meek as potatoes.
Here is the end of winter.
The trees are less horrible now,
and the twilight behind them,
and the glazed shoreline.
You can believe only so long
in the malice of the crooked
and the cold. I think
I'll just sit here awhile
in this strange rock of my own body.
You other rocks, forgive me.
You waves, fall without me.

THE FERRY FROM PATRAS

As we move away the harbor simplifies itself
into one frail line of dock-lights and tavernas
where women are combing their hair
while men say goodnight
the length of the main street.
Not much separates the darkness of air
from the darkness of water:
the creased moonlight, faded altar
of the harbor, the few of us
still watching from the deck.

The engine literally groans deep in the ship
as we move away. The wind increases.
The shoreline tapers into memory.
As if by some signal of ours
the night joins itself like a skull
Even the worst tourists among us
feel more than we deserve to feel,
this strange lace riding over the water.

THE WOMAN ON THE
ROAD TO KAMARI

I could never walk like that, never
tighten my scarf with such finality,
or wear such a constant shawl
of darkness. I could never
tap my cane like a clock
along the cobbles, or learn
to separate the herbs of downfall
from the everlasting ones.
I can only say *good morning*
and *good evening* in Greek.
In between them, the gulls
swing and lapse into the surf,
the sand backslides and rattles.
I could never learn to distinguish
between the true breast
of the local goddess,
and all the ordinary stones
scattered over the mountain.
And although the woman's eyes
are lifted briefly
from the same deep pool
as my own,
I could never summon the nerve
to walk like that, body bent
into the world's oldest question,
carried up the mountain,
death after death.

THE BOMBERS,
A GREEK LOVE TALE

The roar of the American bombers
strafes the beach at Santorini.
If sound has a shadow
it's nearly a minute's worth
of darkness the jets cast
over the half-cocked eyes,
the oiled breasts, glitter
of black sand, wave-tip,
the sweat bead quivering
down the swale of your belly.
No matter how many oceans
or alphabets we cross,
no matter how carefully
we cover our tracks
with money, something
always seems to find us,
if only this brief, dark boom.
The Greeks who lived here
believed Apollo was *light*,
although he often descended
with a clanging of arrows
and armor, according to Homer,
like the swift onrush of night.
Sometimes I think there's a stain
much higher than the body,
like a spot in the sun,
or a small black bird
blundering through heaven.
Sometimes I think the bombers

are not even ours.
But even if they are, even
if we are the Greeks now,
as wise and rich and cruel
as they, the jets have passed
over, dwindling towards Crete.
There's barely a remnant
of shadow left in the sky.
Guilt never lasts long here.
Too much water to wash it.
Too many bodies like mine,
oiled and offered up on the sand;
or yours, sleek and glistening
beside me. And there's a point
in the backsliding of the surf
that resembles either the hiss
of a small fire, or the pause
between such deep and violent
kisses, we've come all this way
just to listen,
just to lie here and burn
in the moment between them.

CAPPUCCINO AT THE
MARCONI HOTEL IN VENICE

It's not the preservation you come for,
not the unadulterated, not the chandelier
that perfectly dodged the carnage,
not the thing that survives intact:
the lace-like facade, or the Byzantine
madonna with the fresh tear
on her cheek. It's the resistance,
the stubbornness of decay, not
the invulnerability, but the reluctance,
the slow peel and flake,
the grudging way the stone passes
into odors and fogs.
It's the ages it takes the algae
to map the canal, and how deep
the mussels sink their hooks
before a single piling shudders.
Some places are more like living in a body
than others, and this may be
one of the best things left:
to sit outside the Marconi Hotel
with your cappuccino and knowledge of death,
and drink it slowly,
and watch the rocking blades
of the parked gondolas, and the wind
threading the arch of the Rialto Bridge,
making time pay for every inch
it takes, a wage of human beauty,
this coin of bristling water.

REVISITING THE SISTINE CHAPEL

They've just cleaned the Creation of Man,
God's beard newly whitened, blown
back in a turbulent cloud
as he reaches for the left hand
of Adam, his first mistake,
Adam's left arm, *il sinistro,*
lazily balanced on his knee,
the outline of the serpent
already lounging in the musculature.
The next two panels are shrouded
for the cleaning of the stars and plants.
Across the curtain covering the scaffold
the restorers' shadows slowly move
like moths tiring in a lampshade.

They're working backwards through time,
the way Michelangelo painted the world:
first the flood, then the fall, then Eve
lured from the dreaming Adam,
her hands posed in an attitude
of prayer, or like a child's hands
poised for a first dive; then
the creation of Adam himself,
and only then, exhausted, embittered
by perfect knowledge
of where it all would lead,
did he paint the birth of light,

a fresco barely visible, still uncleaned,
God's robes whirling toward

definition, arms raised, face
upturned, away from the viewer,
though you can see God was older
in the beginning, his beard thin
and feathery, his shoulders stiff.
The chaos from which he lifts him-
self seems almost too much for him.
Foreknowledge weakens. You can see it
from here. An older hand stirs the light
than the hand that nearly touches Adam

in the fresco they've just cleaned,
making it easier to follow Adam's gaze,
originally assumed to rest on God,
but clearly now sweeping past him
to the newly restored figure of Eve
nestled in the crook of the floating
God's arm, her body caught
in the last moment of girlhood,
changing as she turns, changed
by the turning, her hair bundled
much brighter than anyone imagined.

Looking up at the Creation of Man
now that the dust, soot, gum and resin
have been rubbed away, the patchings
and dubious repaintings, it seems clear,

after all the storms and labor,
who will remain as lonely as ever,
the passion of his creatures
already straying from him.
And though it will be decades
before Michelangelo paints the judgment,
it seems clear what stokes the fire—

not anger, or justice, or even jealousy,
but loneliness, God's dilemma,
the reason he fled the void
in the first place, though
the ailment swept in with him
in the folds of his robe
or the billows of his hair,
the thing he must have known
the light would not alter
even as he reached for it,
as if a single straw
could break the back of all that dark,

which is what makes that famous
gap, those newly brightened inches
between the finger of God
and the lounging hand of man,
the reason for the painting,
or the vault of the chapel itself,
or the upturned face of the visitor,

straining to see, wanting to stay,
yet jostled and swept along
by waves of perfect strangers,

as God knew they would become,
even as he reached for Adam
and felt himself stilled, frozen
in mid-flight, where Michelangelo
would later find him, as if already
painted, precious inches away.

THE
JUNIPER
PRIZE

This volume is the twentieth recipient
of the Juniper Prize
presented annually by the
University of Massachusetts Press
for a volume of original poetry.
The prize is named in honor of
Robert Francis (1901–87),
who lived for many years at
Fort Juniper, Amherst, Massachusetts.